This book belongs to

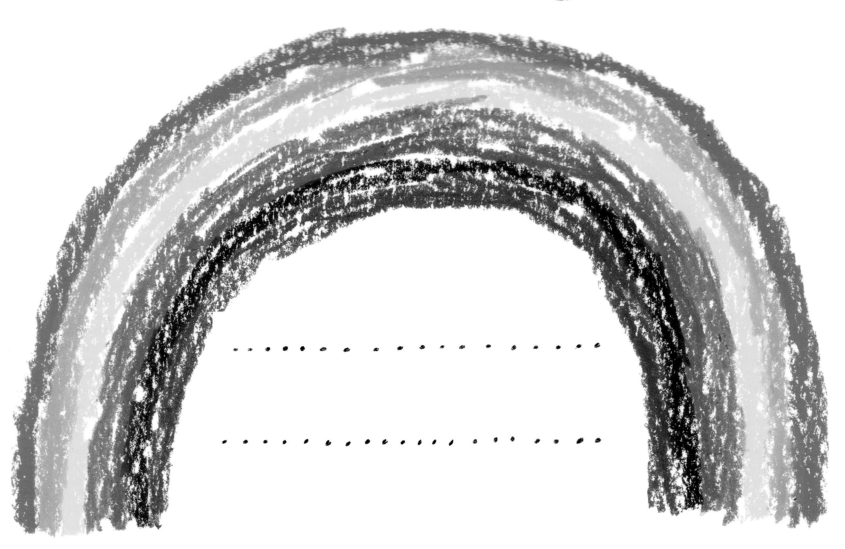

..............................................

..............................................

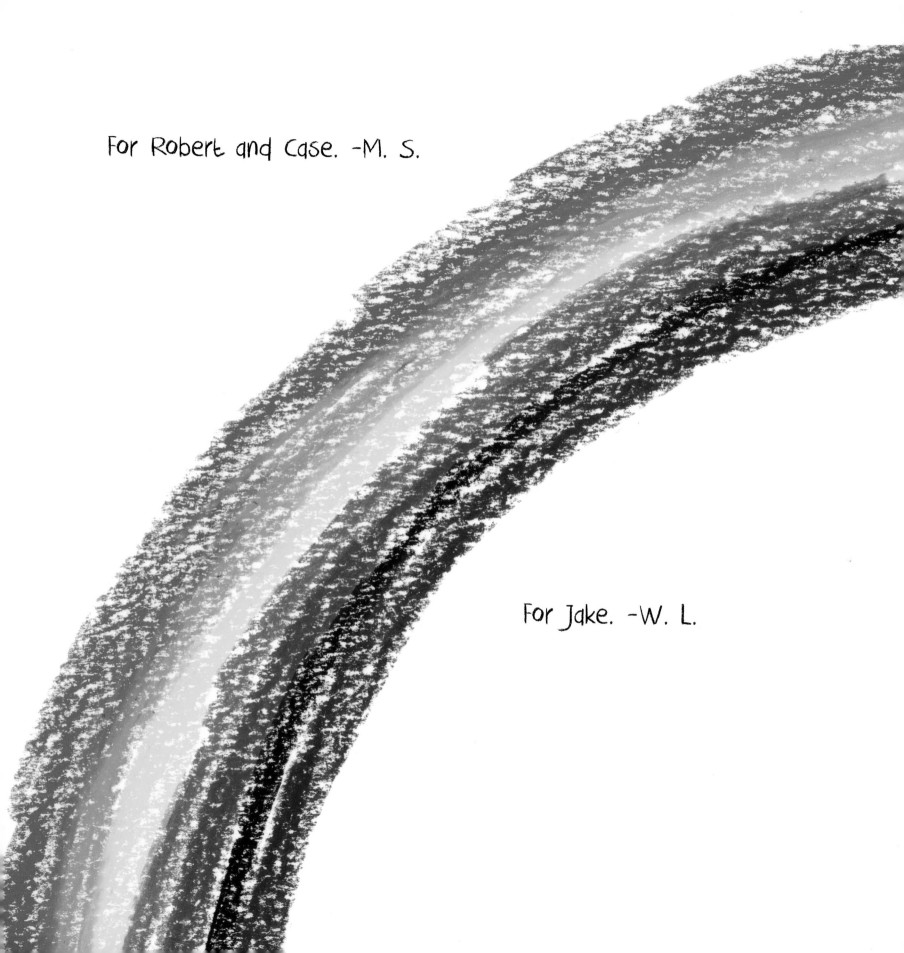

For Robert and Case. -M. S.

For Jake. -W. L.

# How the CRAYONS Saved CHRISTMAS

written by
Monica Sweeney

illustrated by
Wendy Leach

Sky Pony Press
New York

On a cold winter night, in a cozy little cabin in the North Pole, Santa Claus was reading his letters.

The lists of gifts were longer than his fluffy white beard. They were fancier than his magical sleigh!

He decorated his tree,
but it was too crooked!

He asked the elves to help
him bake Christmas cookies,
but they were too busy!

He tried to help them in the workshop,
but nothing came out right.

So he went to see his reindeer, *ho ho ho*,
to get them ready for their Christmas ride.

"Merry Christmas!" He boomed, but the words fell flat.

"On Dasher!" He shouted, but his heart wasn't into it.

"Happy New Year!" He rumbled, but the reindeer didn't even look up.

No matter how he tried, Santa just couldn't find his Christmas spirit.

His fuzzy scarlet suit and his shining gold buckles faded to coal-dust gray.

The twinkly lights on the workshops lost their sparkle.

The bold green trees, the colorful decorations, and the neatly wrapped presents faded bit by bit, until Christmas colors were no more.

"That's it," Santa said with sadness.
"Christmas is canceled!"

He sighed a deep sigh, **_ho ho hummed,_** and sank into his chair.

But tucked far behind the tree was a little box of crayons that Mrs. Claus had picked out just for him. And the crayons still had their colors!

Like little dancing sugar plums,
out jumped seven special crayons!

Santa sat back by the fire, but he didn't feel very warm and didn't feel very merry.

So the crayons made
Christmas cards for Santa.

Some with red and
green trees.

Others with
colorful presents.

They drew and they drew!

The crayons scribbled their hearts out. After each card was done, they floated down, *flutter flutter flutter*, around Santa like snowflakes landing at his feet.

The cards piled higher and higher, but only Santa's boots and red fuzzy pants regained their color.

"We have to do more!" Red and Green cheered.

So the brightest crayon, Yellow, sang a Christmas song for the others to join in. The crayons twirled with delight. They knew just what to do!

The little crayons hopped from rooftop to rooftop.

On the clean white snow, they drew special notes for Santa to see.

Little by little, the North Pole filled in with colors of every kind.

Santa peered out his window, his eyes wide with joy!

Santa and the crayons hopped on the sleigh and soared into the sky. High above the North Pole, Santa saw a world of color made from Christmas spirit.

"Look at everyone celebrating together!" Santa said. "How magical!" His cheeks turned bright pink; his soft suit scarlet again.

His golden buckles twinkled like the lights around town.

"It's just the right time of year to be filled with Christmas cheer!"

Santa and the crayons soared through the sky.

And ever so slowly, the world returned to bright,
sparkling color on a happy Christmas night.

Copyright © 2020 by Hollan Publishing, Inc.

All rights reserved. No part of this book may be reproduced in any manner
without the express written consent of the publisher, except in the case of brief excerpts
in critical reviews or articles. All inquiries should be addressed to
Sky Pony Press, 307 West 36th Street, 11th Floor, New York, NY 10018.

Sky Pony Press books may be purchased in bulk at special discounts for sales promotion,
corporate gifts, fund-raising, or educational purposes. Special editions can also be created to
specifications. For details, contact the Special Sales Department, Sky Pony Press, 307 West 36th
Street, 11th Floor, New York, NY 10018 or info@skyhorsepublishing.com.

Sky Pony® is a registered trademark of Skyhorse Publishing, Inc.®, a Delaware corporation.

Visit our website at www.skyponypress.com.

10 9 8 7 6 5 4 3 2

Manufactured in China, January 2021
This product conforms to CPSIA 2008

Library of Congress Cataloging-in-Publication Data is available on file.

Design by Katie Jennings Campbell
Cover illustration by Wendy Leach

Print ISBN: 978-1-5107-6194-0
Ebook ISBN: 978-1-5107-6389-0